AUNT LULU

Daniel Pinkwater

Macmillan Publishing Company   New York

Macmillan Publishing Company, 866 Third Avenue, New York, NY 10022. Collier Macmillan Canada, Inc.

Printed and bound in Japan. First American Edition 10 9 8 7 6 5 4 3 2 1

The text of this book is set in 14 point Cushing Book. The illustrations are rendered in color markers on paper.

LIBRARY OF CONGRESS CATALOGING-IN-PUBLICATION DATA Pinkwater, Daniel Manus, date. Aunt Lulu/by Daniel Pinkwater.—1st American ed. p. cm. Summary: Tired of working as a librarian in Alaska, Aunt Lulu takes her sled and her fourteen Huskies and moves to Parsippany, New Jersey.
ISBN 0-02-774661-5
[1. Aunts—Fiction. 2. Librarians—Fiction. 3. Dogs—Fiction. 4. Alaska—Fiction. 5. Humorous stories.] I. Title.
PZ7.P6335Au 1988 [E]—dc 19 88-1736 CIP AC

To *good* librarians everywhere

My aunt Lulu is big and strong.
She lives in a house with her pets.
She has a cat.
She has a fish.
She has a bird.
She has a mouse.
She has fourteen dogs.
The dogs are all huskies.
Aunt Lulu got them when she lived in Alaska.
They are sled dogs.

When Aunt Lulu lived in Alaska, she worked in a library.

She would put a lot of books on a sled.

Then she would hook the dogs to the sled.

Then she would say "Mush!"

"Mush!" is what you say to sled dogs to make them go.

"Mush!" she would say.

Then she would call out the dogs' names.

"Mush, Melvin, Louise, Phoebe, Willie, Norman, Hortense, Bruce, Susie, Charles, Teddie, Neddie, Eddie, Freddie, and Sweetie-pie!"

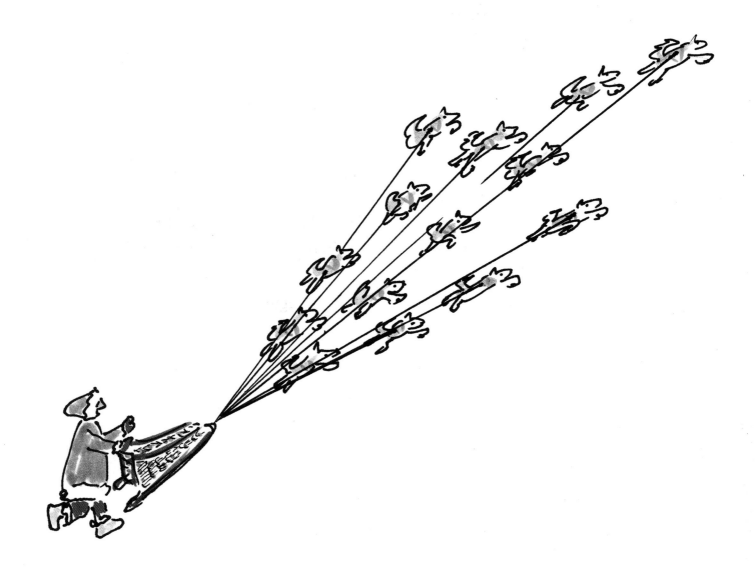

Then Melvin, Louise, Phoebe, Willie, Norman, Hortense, Bruce, Susie, Charles, Teddie, Neddie, Eddie, Freddie, and Sweetie-pie would pull the sled.

Aunt Lulu would drive the sled to the diggings.

The diggings were where the gold miners lived.

When the gold miners saw Aunt Lulu coming, they would stop digging for gold.

"Look! It's Lulu the librarian!" they would shout.

"Look! It's Melvin, Louise, Phoebe, Willie, Norman, Hortense, Bruce, Susie, Charles, Teddie, Neddie, Eddie, Freddie, and Sweetie-pie!"

"Did you bring the books we asked for?" the gold miners would ask.

"Did you bring stories about cowboys?"

"Did you bring stories about pirates?"

"Did you bring stories about sweet little kittens?"

"Did you bring stories about gold miners, and wolves, and freezing to death?"

"Yes, I have brought all the books you wanted," Aunt Lulu would say.

Then she would hand books to the gold miners.

She would collect the books the gold miners had finished reading and put them on the sled.

Then she would turn the sled around.

"Mush, Melvin, Louise, Phoebe, Willie, Norman, Hortense, Bruce, Susie, Charles, Teddie, Neddie, Eddie, Freddie, and Sweetie-pie!" Aunt Lulu would say.

And the dogs would pull the sled back to the library.

Sometimes Aunt Lulu would get lost in the snow.

Sometimes the dogs would lose their way.

Then Aunt Lulu and the dogs would have to sleep out on the trail.

But she was never late coming to collect books, and she always brought the miners the books they asked for.

Aunt Lulu decided it was time to leave Alaska.

She missed her home.

She missed her family.

She missed her friends.

She'd had enough of snow.

She'd had enough of cold.

She'd had enough of miners.

"Those miners are nice fellows," Aunt Lulu said. "But they get boring after a while."

She wrote a letter.

"Get a new librarian," she wrote in the letter. "I am going home."

Then she said good-bye to her dogs.

"Melvin, Louise, Phoebe, Willie, Norman, Hortense, Bruce, Susie, Charles, Teddie, Neddie, Eddie, Freddie, and Sweetie-pie, I am leaving," Aunt Lulu said. "Of course you can't come with me."

All the dogs began to cry.

Sweetie-pie climbed into Aunt Lulu's lap.

He looked at her with sad eyes.

He licked her chin.

"I suppose I could take just *you*," Aunt Lulu said.

Then she looked at all the other dogs. They looked sad.

"Do you all want to come with me?"

The dogs all jumped up and down.

"We will live in New Jersey. Will you like that?"

The dogs smiled and barked.

"It doesn't get as cold as Alaska. Will that be all right?"

The dogs rolled on the ground and waved their feet in the air.

"I guess you want to come with me," Aunt Lulu said.

"Okay. It is settled. We will all go and live in New Jersey."

There was a noise outside Aunt Lulu's house.

It sounded like shouting.

Like shooting.

Also like a moose making moose noises.

"What could that be?" Aunt Lulu said.

She looked out the window.

"It is the miners!" she said. "They have come all the way from the diggings."

The miners knocked on Aunt Lulu's door.

"May we come in?" they asked.

"Certainly," Aunt Lulu said. "This is a nice surprise."

The miners came in to Aunt Lulu's house.

Their names were Nick, Slade, Blackie, Jake, Baldy, Bart, and Spanish Ralph.

"We heard you were going away," Bart said.

"So we came to say good-bye," Nick said.

"We shouted and shot off our guns, like miners do," said Baldy.

"To show you that we like you," said Slade.

"Thank you," Aunt Lulu said. "I also heard moose noises."

"That is your present," Jake said.

"My present? You brought me a moose?"

"No. We brought you a moose *call*," said Spanish Ralph. "You blow it, and moose will answer – if there are any moose around."

"Of course, if you would like to have a moose to take home with you, we could get you one," said Blackie.

"No, thank you," said Aunt Lulu. "A moose call will be very nice. When I am home in New Jersey, I will blow it and remember you all."

The miners blushed, and shuffled their feet, and took their hats off.

"We liked the books you brought us," the miners said.

"Another librarian will bring you books," Aunt Lulu said. "Would you like to have cups of coffee and wolverine stew?"

"Yes, please," the miners said.

Aunt Lulu brought the miners cups of coffee and bowls of wolverine stew.

"Where will you live in New Jersey?" Spanish Ralph asked.

"Parsippany," Aunt Lulu said.

"That's a beautiful place," Baldy said.

"Are you taking the dogs with you?" Jake asked.

"Yes," said Aunt Lulu.

"That's good," Blackie said.

"Yes," said Aunt Lulu.

"The dogs will like living in Parsippany," Slade said.

"I hope so," Aunt Lulu said.

After the miners finished their cups of coffee and bowls of wolverine stew, they all said good-bye to Aunt Lulu and went away.

"Nice men," Aunt Lulu said to herself, "but boring."

When Aunt Lulu came back to live in New Jersey, the first thing she did was come to see us.

It was winter.

There was plenty of snow.

She came to see us in a sled.

She wore a parka lined with fur.

Pulling the sled were Melvin, Louise, Phoebe, Willie, Norman, Hortense, Bruce, Susie, Charles, Teddie, Neddie, Eddie, Freddie, and Sweetie-pie.

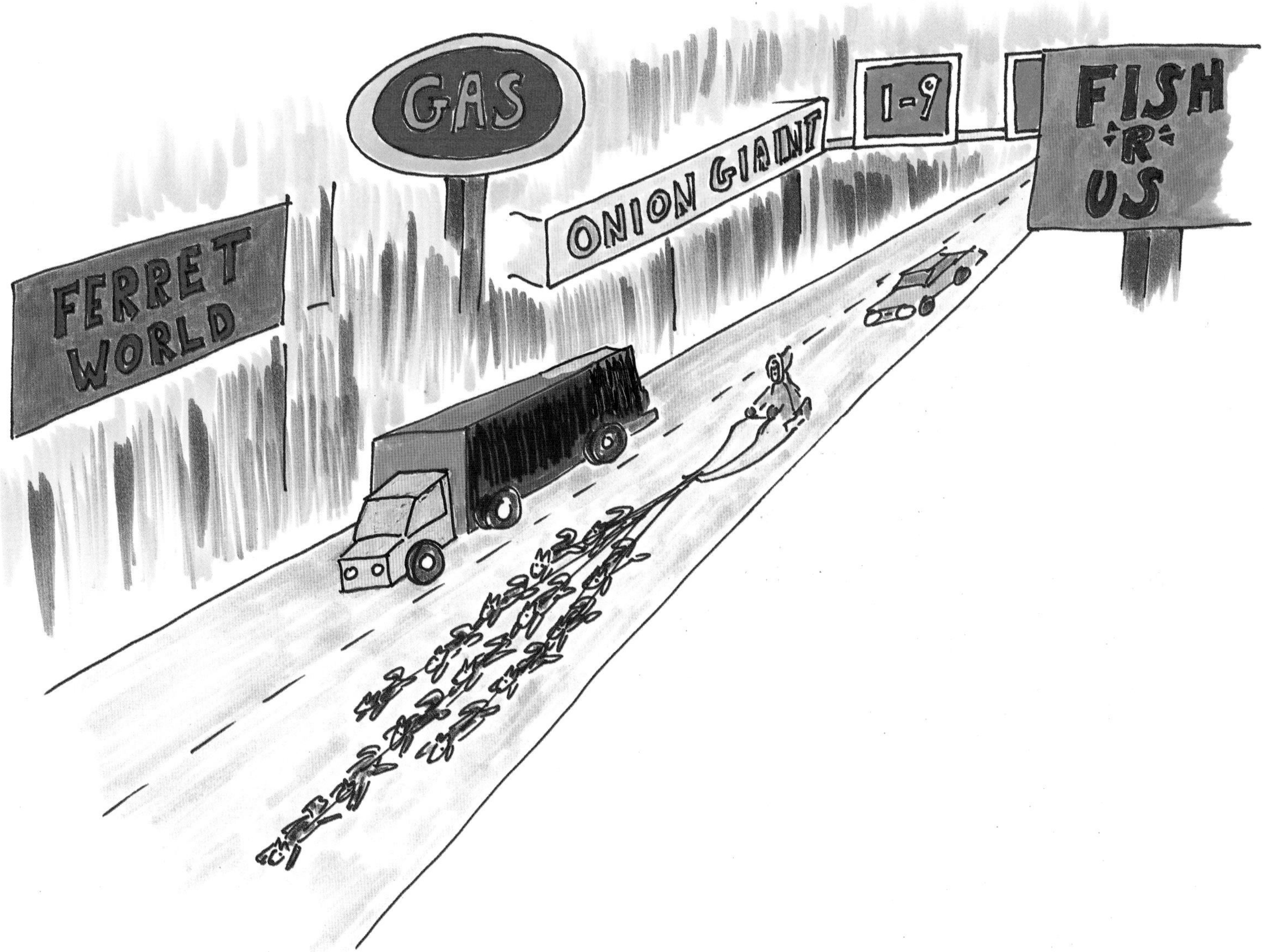
FERRET WORLD
GAS
ONION GIANT
I-9
FISH R US

Aunt Lulu showed me the moose call the miners had given her.

"You may keep this," she said, "but don't blow it outdoors, or moose will come."

"We don't have any moose in Parsippany, New Jersey," my mother said.

"You might have some," Aunt Lulu said. "You don't want them around the house."

"Are you always going to go around in that dogsled?" my mother asked.

"I don't see why not," Aunt Lulu said.

"What will you do in summer?" my mother asked.

"When summer comes, we'll have to see," Aunt Lulu said.

"Don't you think a car would be better?" my mother asked.

"Not while I have this perfectly good dog team," Aunt Lulu said.

Summer came.

Aunt Lulu came to see us.

She had put wheels on her dogsled.

She was not wearing her fur-lined parka.

She had a dress on.

She had sunglasses with pink frames.

Melvin, Louise, Phoebe, Willie, Norman, Hortense, Bruce, Susie, Charles, Teddie, Neddie, Eddie, Freddie, and Sweetie-pie all had sunglasses with pink frames too.

"We like this warm weather," Aunt Lulu said.

Aunt Lulu still lives in Parsippany, New Jersey.

In winter she drives the dogsled all over town.

In summer she drives the dogsled with wheels on it.

Winter and summer, she wears her sunglasses with pink frames.

And Melvin, Louise, Phoebe, Willie, Norman, Hortense, Bruce, Susie, Charles, Teddie, Neddie, Eddie, Freddie, and Sweetie-pie wear their sunglasses with pink frames too.